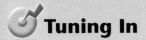
Tuning In

Where Do All the Puddles Go? is an expl... a sequence of steps; the contents page ... each stage of the explanation.

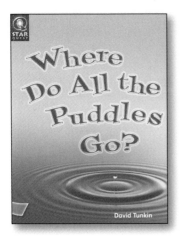

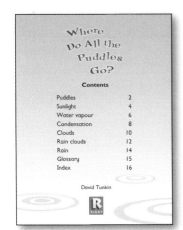

The front cover

What do you notice about the heading?

Speaking and Listening

Why do you think it is sometimes useful to make the heading a question?

The back cover

What does the blurb tell us?

What type of book is this? (a science book, information book)

Contents

Read the headings in the list of contents.

Look at the heading for page 8.

Let's work out what the word is by looking at the first two syllables (con/den).

The letters 'tion' make a 'shun' sound.

READ

Read pages 2 and 3

Purpose: to find out how puddles are formed.

PAUSE

Pause at page 3

How are puddles made?

Can you give me the answer in just two or three words?

Puddles

What happens when it rains?

When it rains, drops of water form puddles on the ground.

Have you ever wanted to know what happens to the water in a puddle?

Read pages 4 and 5

Purpose: to find out what sunlight does to the puddles.

Pause at page 5

On paper or whiteboards draw what happens when the sun comes out.

Speaking and Listening

Let's look at what you have drawn.

Explain your drawing to us.

Does it look like a diagram or a picture?

Have you put in arrows or words?

If not, try again, to make it more like a science diagram. (Don't erase it.)

Sunlight

What happens when it stops raining?

When it stops raining and the sun comes out,
the puddles start to dry up.
The sun shines onto the puddles. Sunlight
is warm, so it heats the water in the puddles.

Read pages 6 and 7

Purpose: to find out where the water goes.

Pause at page 7

What two words were difficult on page 6?

Let's break them into syllables to read them correctly.

Speaking and Listening

Why are 'evaporates' and 'water vapour' in bold type?

Turn to page 15 and find the glossary.

How is a glossary useful?

Water vapour

What happens when water gets warm?

Heat from the sun can make water evaporate. When water **evaporates**, it turns into water vapour. We cannot see **water vapour**, but it is in the air.

Read pages 8 and 9

Purpose: to discover what 'condensation' means.

Pause at page 9

What is 'condensation'?

Let's look in the glossary to check we are right.

Condensation

What happens when water rises?

Water vapour in the air cools down as it rises. As it cools down, the water vapour in the air turns back into tiny drops of water. This is called **condensation**.

Read pages 10 and 11

Purpose: to find out where the water drops go.

Pause at page 11

Go back to the diagram you drew earlier, and add this information. Remember to use arrows instead of lots of words.

Speaking and Listening

Explain your diagram to us.

What are the scientific words that you need to explain your diagram?

Clouds

What happens to water drops?

As the water drops get bigger, they group together and form a cloud.

The clouds are blown across the sky by the wind. More water vapour joins the clouds from other puddles, and from rivers and the sea.

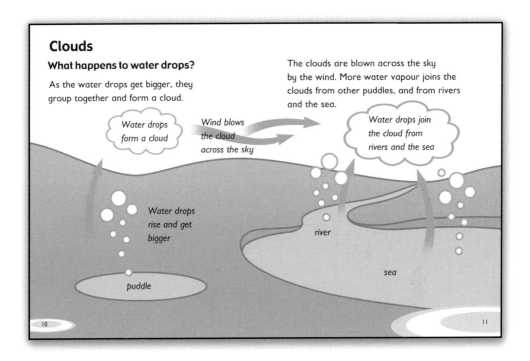

Read pages 12 and 13

Purpose: to find out what makes a rain cloud.

Pause at page 13

What do you expect to read about on the next page?

Rain clouds

What happens to clouds?

As more water vapour joins a cloud, the drops in the cloud get bigger. Then the cloud gets bigger and darker and becomes a rain cloud.

READ

Read page 14

Purpose: to find out what happens to the clouds.

PAUSE

Pause at page 14

Add this extra information to your diagram.

Speaking and Listening

Explain your diagram to us.

What words does the text use to describe the whole thing starting again?

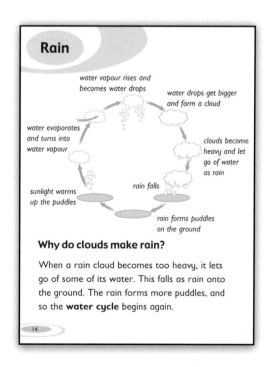

READ

Read page 15

Purpose: to check the meaning of the scientific words.

PAUSE

Pause at page 15

Why do you think there is a glossary in this book?

Do all non-fiction books need glossaries?

Which type of books do you need a glossary in?

Read page 16

Purpose: to use an index.

Pause at page 16

On which pages will you find 'puddle'?

Speaking and Listening

How is an index different to a glossary?